THIS BOOK
BELONGS TO

....

THE QUEEN'S SWANS

WRITTEN & ILLUSTRATED
BY LAURA WILSON

One day this queen was VERY bored, adventure she did seek.

She gave the royal swans a note, to meet her the next week.

The swans all came in hats and jewels. They sang, they danced, they ate.

The queen went for a walk with them, straight OUT the big gold gate!

As Queenie upped
and swooped behind
her swans into the
skies!

In the sky they went 'til they were
nowhere to be seen.

Over chimneys, pools and houses, the Queen had quite the view.

Then higher up the swans did fly, the Queen called "how'd you do?".

The streets were lined with people,
each one stood still in shock.

The news was go go go,

with people saying what they'd seen.

Queenie held on tighter as they flew out across the ocean.

They even saw the desert as they dashed off through the sky.

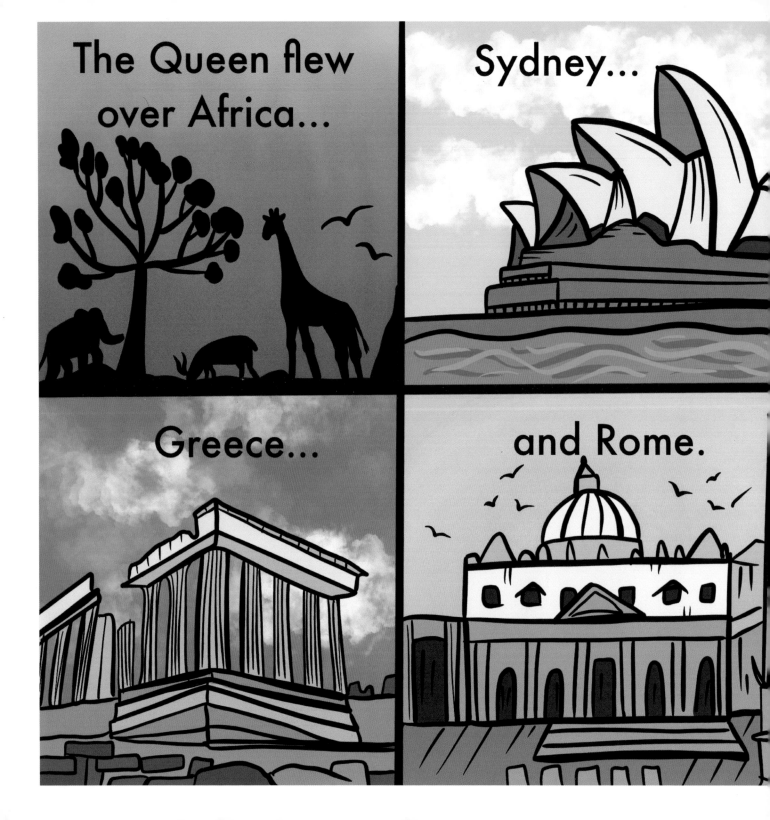

The cups of tea, her corgis, friends and family she did miss.

Sometimes she would write to them and sign off with a kiss.

So once again they flew until her palace was in sight.

"At last" she said, "we're home again, the swans can rest their wings".

"But now I'm home for good this time, let's have a cup of tea".

The Queen was home and all felt right, she'd had the perfect quest.

Nothing felt as good as home, it really was the best!

Printed in Great Britain
by Amazon